The
NEW BABY

by Ruth and Harold Shane

illustrated by Eloise Wilkin

A GOLDEN BOOK • NEW YORK

Western Publishing Company, Inc., Racine, Wisconsin 53404

MNOPQRST

One day, a big green truck stopped in front of
Mike's house. The deliveryman took a large box
from the truck and carried it to the porch, where
Mike was playing.

What could it be? It wasn't Christmas, so it
couldn't be a Christmas present. It wasn't a lawn
mower. Daddy had a lawn mower. It wasn't a new
tricycle. Mike had a new red tricycle.

"Hello," Mike said to the deliveryman.

The deliveryman said, "Hello, there."

"Is that for us?" asked Mike.

"Yes," replied the deliveryman. He rang the doorbell, then waited for someone to answer.

"What's in it?" asked Mike.

"It's a buggy."

Mike wondered what a buggy could be.

Mummy came to the door. "Bring the box right in," she said.

The deliveryman put the box by the window. Then he went back to the truck and drove away.

Mike looked at the big box. "What's a buggy, Mummy?" he asked.

Daddy came in before Mummy had time to answer. "Aha!" he said. "Here's our new buggy."

"What *is* a buggy?" asked Mike again.

"It's a little bed on wheels," said Daddy, opening the box. "You've seen them lots of times. It's for the new baby."

For a minute Mike didn't say anything.

"Whose baby?" he asked at last.

"Ours," Daddy said. "Before long, we're going to have a new baby."

Mike couldn't believe it!

"A *baby!*" he said excitedly. "What will it be like? Will it be a little girl? Will it be a boy? When is it coming here? Will it have red hair like Susie next door?"

"Hold on a minute!" said Daddy, laughing. "We don't know those things yet. We can only guess. It'll be a surprise."

A few days later, Mike had another surprise. Aunt Pat came to visit. "She's going to help us take care of the baby," said Daddy.

At supper, Mike asked, "Who'll bring the baby?"

Mummy said, "No one will. I'll go to the hospital soon, and the baby will be born there."

That night Mike woke up. It was still dark outside, and the hall light was on. Aunt Pat was in the hall in her bathrobe. Mummy and Daddy were up, too.

"Where are you going?" Mike asked.

Mummy kissed Mike and smiled. "I'm going to the hospital for our baby," she said. "I'll bring it home very soon."

In the morning, Mike helped Aunt Pat. He brought out the cornflakes. He helped set the table. He carried the milk from the refrigerator. Then he ate every bit of his breakfast.

The telephone rang. Mike got there first. It was Daddy calling.

Daddy said, "Mike, you have a beautiful baby sister!"

"Ohhh!" said Mike, handing the telephone to Aunt Pat. "Maybe I could run and tell Mrs. Blair."

"Of course you may," Aunt Pat told him. So Mike ran next door as fast as he could.

Before long, Daddy came home. He boosted Mike into the air and then went into the house.

Just then a big green truck stopped in front of the house. The deliveryman took a big box from his truck. He was bringing it to Mike's house. What could it be?

It wasn't Christmas yet, so it couldn't be a Christmas present. It couldn't be a lawn mower. Daddy still had a lawn mower. And it couldn't be a tricycle. Mike still had his red tricycle. Could it be another buggy?

Mike ran up the steps. He didn't even wait to say hello to the deliveryman. He went looking for Daddy and Aunt Pat. He was so excited.

"Daddy! Aunt Pat! Are we going to have *another* baby?"

"What?" asked Daddy.

"I hardly think so," said Aunt Pat. "At least, not for a while. Why do you ask?"

"Well," said Mike, "the deliveryman is here with another box. When he brought one before, the baby was born!"

Daddy laughed and said, "This is a surprise for *you*, Mike. Let's go and get the package."

The deliveryman was at the door.

"Hello," Mike said.

The deliveryman said, "Hello, there."

"That's for *me*," Mike told him, pointing to the package. Daddy and the deliveryman carried the big box upstairs.

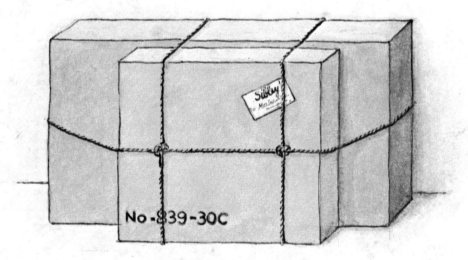

No -339-30C

Mike ran upstairs behind them. He and Daddy opened the box—it was really two boxes tied together—and there was a big, new bed!

"For *me!*" cried Mike.

Mike and Daddy put it together. Mike was very happy and said, "Now the baby can have my little bed, can't she?"

He wanted very much to see the baby. It seemed a very long time that he had to wait. Aunt Pat and Daddy went to see Mummy and the baby every day.

Mike and Daddy talked about what the baby's name should be. Daddy said Mummy had suggested naming her Pat, after Aunt Pat.

"I like that," said Mike.

"So do I," said Daddy.

So it was decided.

Mike kept wondering, "What will the baby look like? When will Mummy bring her home?"

Then one day, Daddy went to drive Mummy and little Pat home from the hospital. Mike sat on the steps and waited. A green car came along. It was not Mike's car. A yellow car came along. It was not Mike's car, either.

Then a blue car turned the corner. That *was* Mike's car.

"Hello, Mike!" Mummy called. "We're home!"

Mike ran down the sidewalk to the car. Daddy got out first. He gave Mike an extra-high boost into the air. Then he turned to Mummy and little Pat.

Mummy got out of the car, handed the baby to Daddy, and gave Mike a kiss and a hug. She told him how glad she was to be home.

Aunt Pat came out of the house. Mrs. Blair and Susie came over from the house next door. Everyone wanted to see little Pat.

But Mike wanted to see her most of all. He looked. She had tiny hands, and she had blue eyes. She had soft, wispy hair.

When Mike, Aunt Pat, Daddy, little Pat, and Mummy were inside, Mike asked, "May I hold our baby?"

"Of course you may," Mummy said.

So Mike sat on the couch. He sat way back and held the baby just right. How proud Mike was! It was wonderful to have a baby, he thought.